STAGE

School

CHLOE LEARNS A LESSON

STAGE
School

CHLOE LEARNS A LESSON

Holly Skeet

BLOOMSBURY

First published in Great Britain in 2007 by Bloomsbury Publishing Plc
36 Soho Square, London, W1D 3QY

A CIP catalogue record of this book is available from the British Library

ISBN 978 0 7475 8719 4

All papers used by Bloomsbury Publishing are natural, recyclable products made
from wood grown in well-managed forests. The manufacturing processes conform
to the environmental regulations of the country of origin.

Typeset by Dorchester Typesetting Group Ltd
Printed in Great Britain by Clays Ltd, St Ives Plc

1 3 5 7 9 10 8 6 4 2

www.bloomsbury.com

For Jon, Tom,
William and Robin

Chapter One

CHLOE LIVES HER DREAM

'Have you got everything?' Mrs Ford asked again anxiously.

'Yes, Mum.' Chloe was hardly listening – she was too excited, and anyway, it was at least the third time Mum had asked her.

Mum was giving Chloe a lift because it was the first day. Chloe had wanted to go on her own, but when she'd suggested it, Mum had been quite upset.

She'd tried to explain that she'd worked out the route, but Mum and Dad weren't having it. She knew why – they were so proud of her for getting into the school, and they wanted to be a part of it. She was used to them being involved. They came to all her shows – her dad videoed them all, and any-one who came to the house was lucky to get away without being shown Chloe aged three in her dance school pageant, dressed as a daffodil and stealing the show as usual.

Chloe's dad suddenly popped his head out of the kitchen. 'You could take the video camera –'

'*No!*' Chloe squawked in horror. No way! She couldn't imagine anything worse – all the cool people at Lane's walking past and sniggering as her mum videoed her going up the steps. 'No, Dad. No video, no photos, no hugging, and if we don't leave now I'm going on the train without even Mum, 'cause otherwise we're going to be late.'

As she'd expected, that put her mum in an imme-diate panic. She ran out of the door without even bringing the car keys, she was so desperate for

Chloe not to be late. Chloe followed her, grinning, and carrying her rucksack, her bag of dance clothes, and her mum's handbag.

Chloe was too excited to be scared, even though this was her first day. She'd been desperate to go somewhere like Lane's since she'd been six and found out that stage schools existed. Then last year her dance teacher had told her about the audition for Lane's and she knew that it would be perfect. Classes in ballet, tap, modern dance, singing and drama (and normal boring subjects like maths as well, of course) and you got to be represented by the Marcia Lane Agency. They'd be sending her to fantastic auditions all the time! The school had a world-wide reputation – people came from abroad to go to it. Going to Lane's was Chloe's dream come true. She couldn't wait to be there!

Somehow, seeing the big white stone building that housed the Marcia Lane School of Drama and Dance made Chloe feel slightly less confident. She'd been there before, of course, for her audition, but that had been during the holidays, and the crowd of

students pouring in the doors and milling around on the steps made a big difference. Chloe knew there were only about a hundred and fifty students, but they all seemed to be arriving right now . . . For the first time, Chloe felt new, and rather small, as she and her mum walked up Abbeyfield Road towards the school. She even felt glad that Lane's had a school uniform. She'd been very disappointed, when she'd first found this out. Chloe had assumed that at a stage school you'd be able to wear whatever you wanted. But the information they'd been sent about the school said that the uniform was really important, and everyone had to wear it, even the oldest students. Now though, Chloe was thankful to be wearing the smart grey skirt and blazer, burgundy sweater, and burgundy and silver stripy tie – at least she looked like she belonged. If she'd had her own clothes on, she might have worn something that wasn't quite right . . .

Chloe shook herself, and marched determinedly towards the big glass doors. What on *earth* was she thinking? For a start, there was no way that with her

perfect dress sense she would *ever* wear something that wasn't completely cool. And since when had she cared what anyone else thought anyway? She totally disapproved of school uniform, and she was going to tell somebody so, the first opportunity she got.

Chloe's temporary grumpiness disappeared as she and her mum went up the steps to the school. She couldn't help listening in on a fascinating conversation:

'So the casting director said, "Can you swim?" And I said of course I could, I was a really good swimmer –'

'Amy Martin, you sink to the bottom of the pool every week!'

'I know!' the curly-haired girl giggled. 'I don't know what I'll do if I get the part. Miss Jones'll have to give me extra lessons or something – she's gonna kill me!'

Chloe gazed enviously at Amy, who looked about thirteen, just a couple of years older than her. She sounded so calm about it all! Chloe could

understand exactly what Amy meant though. If she was lucky enough to get a professional audition, she would swear blind she could swim, ride, even *juggle* if that's what they wanted. Plenty of time to worry afterwards!

Chapter Two

THE MOST IMPORTANT TWO HOURS EVER

Chloe smiled to herself as she and her mum went through the glass doors — it felt familiar, like this place belonged to her. She'd known Lane's was right ever since she came for the audition. Her dance teacher had brought her, along with Sophie, another girl from her class. Chloe and Sophie had been friendly rivals for years — they always fought for the best role in the Christmas show, and Chloe almost

always won. But she liked Sophie, and thought she was a really good dancer. It had been so nice to have somebody she knew doing the audition too!

That had been back in January, a whole nine months ago, but Chloe didn't think she'd ever forget it. Mrs Rose had taken her and Sophie on the train, and they'd been giggly and over-excited the whole way there. It was so hard to believe that the next two hours might mean the rest of their lives were totally different. Once they'd seen the school building, and the big gold sign over the door, they suddenly shut up.

Chloe narrowed her lips into a thin line. There was *no way* she was going to mess this up – she had to show the selection committee what she could do. She glanced at Sophie, ready to give her a 'Let's do this!' grin. But then the grin slipped – Sophie had actually gone *green*. Chloe thought people only did that in books. 'Are you OK?' she muttered worriedly, and Sophie shook her head. 'I think I'm going to be sick!' she gasped.

Mrs Rose steered her into the school. 'You stay right there, Chloe,' she called, shooing Sophie towards the toilets. 'Back in a minute!'

It was more like ten minutes. Chloe wasn't too worried to start with – Sophie was just nervous, and nerves took some people that way; she'd be OK in no time. But it was scary, standing there on her own, clutching her dance things and watching everyone else streaming by with their parents or teachers. What if they forgot about her? *What if she missed her audition?* The letter had been so strict – if you were late, you didn't get another chance. She supposed it was like professional auditions – no one was going to wait around for you if you couldn't be bothered to get there on time. Chloe was looking anxiously towards the loos, and wondering if she should go and see what was going on, when Mrs Rose and Sophie emerged. She beamed at them, expecting her friend to be back to normal.

Sophie wasn't. She wasn't green any more – her pretty fair skin was grey instead, and even her

15

bouncy blonde curls were limp. She was leaning against Mrs Rose and she hardly seemed able to walk, let alone dance her way through a strenuous audition. Chloe tried not to let her dismay show in her face – that was the last thing Sophie needed – but it was difficult.

'Sorry to leave you in the lurch like that. Right! Let's get on and sign you both in,' said Mrs Rose sounding stressed.

Was Sophie going to audition like *that*? Chloe didn't say anything though, just followed as they headed down the corridor. When they stopped in a queue of other girls and boys, all waiting to be ticked off on a massive list, she had a chance to speak to Sophie.

'Are you feeling better?' she asked anxiously.

'Mmmm. A bit. Sorry. Must have really put you off!' Sophie smiled weakly.

'No, I was just worried about you – you've never had anything like this before, at shows or anything.'

'I always get really nervous,' Sophie gulped. 'I suppose this is worse because it's just so important.

Oh Chloe, I'm not sure I can do the audition feeling like this!'

To be honest, she didn't really think Sophie could either, but she could hardly say that, could she? 'It'll be OK,' she said firmly. 'The adrenalin will take over. You know what Mrs Rose says – just smile and concentrate on your music, and you'll remember what to do.'

But inside she had a horrible feeling that Sophie's once-in-a-lifetime chance had already gone . . .

Once the secretary had signed them in, everyone was herded into a big waiting room. They'd all been given numbers that they had to pin on to their dance clothes. Chloe and Sophie were thirty-six and thirty-seven. Chloe couldn't believe how many people there were auditioning. She knew Lane's only took about thirty students a year – and this was just one of four days of auditions!

A harassed-looking woman was explaining the audition routine. 'We're going to see you for dance in groups of ten – ballet first, and then tap. Then we'll move on to hearing your voice pieces and

doing some improvisation to see your drama skills after that. So, can the first group, numbers one to ten, follow me to the changing rooms? Parents and teachers wait here, please.'

Chloe watched enviously as the first ten people got up, anxiously searching for bags and saying goodbye to their parents. One of the girls looked almost as ill as Sophie. Chloe wished that she could have been in the first group. She knew that once the audition started she would feel fine, but the waiting was awful. She was sure she could feel her heart thumping all the way round her body.

It was another half an hour before their group was called to go and change. Chloe was relieved, but she saw the colour fade out of Sophie's face again as their numbers were called, and she dropped her bag, as though her fingers were so numb she could hardly feel them.

Chloe sprayed her hair with a water mister to get the dark-red curls to behave and fought it into a bun. Then she examined herself carefully in the mirror. She was wearing her normal dance clothes –

pale pink tights and the dark pink leotard that all Mrs Rose's students wore. She wrapped her pink cardigan over the top.

'Is your friend OK?' a voice asked shyly. Chloe turned to see a tiny Chinese girl with perfect creamy skin. She was looking at Sophie, who was sitting on the bench and staring at nothing, her face still a pale shade of grey.

'I don't think so,' Chloe murmured. 'It's such bad luck – she's a brilliant dancer, and she has a fantastic singing voice, but I just don't think they'll see any of it.' She was trying to pin the number on to the back of her leotard as she spoke, and the Chinese girl giggled.

'Here, let me. You'll put your back out twisting like that.'

'Thanks. I can do yours for you if you like. Then I think I'd better try and get Soph back on this planet – she looks totally out of it.'

The other girl turned round for Chloe to pin on her label. 'Mmmm. Good luck.'

Just then the secretary popped her head round

the door. 'Two minutes, girls, and I'll be back to take you into your ballet audition.'

The two girls exchanged panicked glances and then looked at Sophie, who hadn't even noticed the announcement.

'I'll help. I can do her hair while you try and get her back with us.'

'That would be fab,' Chloe said gratefully. The girl had already started to work Sophie's curls into a French plait, and seemed pleased to have something to do. Chloe sat down on the bench next to her friend, and took one of her hands. It was freezing.

'Sophie, listen. We're about ready to go into the audition, are you sure you're up for it?'

Sophie managed a small smile, but that was all. Chloe put an arm round her shoulders. Sophie felt so tense. How was she ever going to loosen up and dance?

The door opened again. 'Everyone follow me to the studio, please!'

This was it!

The studio was enormous, with a sprung wooden floor, and mirrors all round the walls. The audition panel were sitting at a table down one side, watching interestedly as they came in. Chloe remembered Mrs Rose saying that the audition started as soon as you walked in the door. She tried to stand confidently and keep her head up.

One of the school's ballet teachers took them through a warm-up, walking round the group as they did their stretches. Occasionally she asked someone to lengthen their leg, or pushed down on a shoulder to see how supple someone was. When she came to Chloe, she seemed to be standing there for ages, and Chloe had to concentrate on even remembering to breathe. But she didn't say anything. As they got into line at the barre, Chloe was glad to see that the ritual of the familiar exercises seemed to have brought Sophie back to the real world. She didn't look fantastic, but she was moving with something of her usual grace.

Chloe felt herself beginning to relax as the

instructions continued. She could do all this – she *loved* doing all this! Unconsciously she began to smile as they dropped into a series of deep *pliés*, and as the ballet teacher passed her she murmured an appreciative 'Nice!' Chloe glowed, and felt the concentrated envy of nine other people burning into her back. After the barre work, they had to learn a short sequence of steps to dance across the centre of the room – and that was it. Chloe felt confused as she saw the clock on her way out. That had taken half an hour? It didn't seem possible.

They were whisked back to the changing room to put on leggings and T-shirts for tap, and then off to another studio, and yet another scary panel of judges. But if anything, the tap session was even more fun, playing a weird kind of follow-my-leader round the studio, trying to keep up with the teacher. Half of them were in hysterics by the end, and Chloe completely forgot about the judges until she was heading out of the door.

'Right! Change into your track pants and put a sweater on, then follow the signs to the cafeteria.

There are snacks out for you there. Then it's singing. We'll call you one at a time for that.'

Chloe fell on the biscuits and drinks as though she hadn't seen food for weeks. Even Sophie nibbled on a digestive, but she was looking down.

'Feeling better?' Chloe nudged her.

'Yeah. But it's too late! I was useless in the ballet, totally wooden. They'll never want me.'

'You've still got the singing and the drama – you could pull it off,' put in the Chinese girl, who had come over by now and was smiling encouragingly. 'Ouch – did you hear that? How flat is *that* girl!' They could hear the singing auditions going on in a room close by.

'You'll be better than that, Soph!' Chloe agreed.

Sophie grinned. 'Well, it wouldn't be hard! I just feel like I've already messed it up though.'

'Never give up,' said Chloe firmly.

'Bethany Cheung!' a voice called.

'That's me!'

Chloe had seen how good Bethany was at ballet,

and tap – she had fantastic timing. What was her voice like?

It was good – better than good. She and Sophie sat awestruck as the silvery notes floated down the corridor.

'I might as well go home now!' Sophie sighed. 'She's awesome!'

Chapter Three
OLD HANDS AND NEW FACES

Chloe looked round the hallway again, remembering the audition and poor Sophie's green face. She'd been right – she hadn't got in, even though she said they'd sent her a really nice letter. Sophie was going to her local secondary school, but she swore she was keeping on with dance, and she was going to do as much drama and music as she could at school. Maybe she'd be able to do a drama course when she

was sixteen. Chloe had meant to grab Bethany and ask for her email after the drama part of the audition, but everyone was sent off a few at a time as the audition finished, and she only saw her in the distance. So she had no idea whether the pretty Chinese girl would be at Lane's or not. Chloe guessed she would though – unless Bethany had some kind of mystery acting disability, like she turned into a muppet as soon as she tried to move on a stage, there was no way that voice and that dancing weren't getting in.

'I wonder where we need to go,' murmured Chloe's mum, looking around as boys and girls in the grey and burgundy uniforms surged past her.

'All I have to do is sign in and go to my classroom, Mum, like it said in the letter. You can leave me to it.'

'But Chloe, all these people – don't you want me to come with you?' Her mum sounded worried, and a bit disappointed, but Chloe really wanted her to leave! As soon as she was gone, she could be a real Lane's student – not just a new girl hanging around

with her mum like a baby. Chloe really wanted to get on with it. She gave her mum a big hug. 'Thanks for driving me, it was really sweet. But I'll be fine on my own now, honestly. I'll tell you all about it tonight.'

She practically shooed her mum out of the door. After waving her off, she turned back into the school hall and sighed happily, gazing all around and taking it in. She was here at last!

Just then, a tall woman with fabulous long dark hair flung open the glass door, and marched in as though she expected everyone to rush to meet her. As soon as she was through the door, she stopped and posed, waiting for people to notice her. She was very familiar somehow, as though Chloe had seen her lots of times before, but she just couldn't quite place her. Behind the woman, and looking as though she would rather be almost anywhere else, was a girl who looked very like her. She had the same nearly black hair and very white skin, but none of the commanding presence. The girl was in Lane's uniform, so Chloe guessed this was another new girl.

'Excuse me!' The tall woman had spotted a member of staff, and was summoning her over. And as soon as Chloe heard her voice, she realised who she was. Well, she couldn't remember her name exactly, but she was an actress. One of those people who was always on TV in a murder mystery series, or doing an ad for cream cheese. Chloe watched interestedly, thinking that she must remember to tell her dad – he loved that sort of detective thing.

'This is my daughter, Lily Ferrars. You know who I am, of course?' The woman gave a very artificial laugh – 'Marina Ferrars.' She said it as though she expected the teacher to whip out an autograph book. 'Lily is starting at Lane's this term – following in her mother's footsteps.' She clasped the girl to her in a dramatic hug, and Lily looked as though she wanted to die. 'I gather we have to *sign in*.' She made it sound like this was totally beneath her, as though famous actresses really shouldn't have to do this sort of thing.

The teacher was looking decidedly unimpressed. She just smiled at Lily, and then pointed out the big

pink arrows with 'new students' written on them. 'You just need to follow those. I'll see you later on, Lily. I'm Ms Driver – I'll be teaching you tap.' Then she whisked off as fast as she could, obviously wanting to get well out of Marina Ferrars' way.

Chloe watched, fascinated, as Marina Ferrars staged a dramatic goodbye scene with her daughter in the middle of the hall, going on and on about how wonderful it was for Lily to be here, where her mother's career had started, and how she was 'taking her first steps on the road to stardom'. She actually said that! Lily just stood there, staring at the floor, but her mother didn't seem to care – the little act wasn't for her benefit at all. Unfortunately, nobody really seemed to be appreciating it all that much, although there were quite a few whispers along the lines of 'What was that stupid thing about a murder she was in last year?'

Chloe suddenly realised that she'd better get on and find where she was meant to be. 'Follow the pink arrows,' Ms Driver had said. She set off down the corridor, feeling guilty. After watching that great

drama, Chloe suddenly felt she shouldn't have sent her own mum off so quickly, it was mean of her. She was so lucky to have normal parents who didn't do awful things like that! Even Dad's video camera obsession didn't seem so embarrassing now.

Chloe stopped short. Thinking about Mum she hadn't been concentrating. Now she'd gone round a corner without looking for a pink arrow. Where was she? Chloe gulped as a sudden tide of panic rushed over her. She would give anything to have Mum with her now – they'd still be lost, because Mum had a worse sense of direction than a hamster, but at least she wouldn't be on her own!

A friendly-looking man in track pants and a Lane's fleece came round the corner the other way and stopped just before he bumped into Chloe. 'I told them they needed another arrow on this corner. Lost, aren't you? Don't worry, you're about the fifth lost first year I've found this morning. Back round the corner and straight on.' Chloe was still standing there looking gormless, so he gave her a gentle shove in the right direction, and she scurried off.

The same secretary who'd been organising the auditions was now signing in the new students. Chloe had obviously got more lost than she'd realised, because dark-haired Lily was there registering in front of her, now without her embarrassing mother. She still looked upset though. Chloe decided that she'd go and say hello to her once she'd been ticked off the list.

'Right, you need one of these.' The secretary handed her a folder. 'List of staff, the school rules, map of the school – *very* important.'

Chloe blushed. Did everyone know she'd got lost?

'Everything you need should be in there. Now you need to go up these stairs to your classroom. Just keep following the pink arrows.'

That's what they said last time, Chloe thought to herself as she set off. She looked around for Lily, but she seemed to have already met up with some friends. At least, three older girls were certainly talking to her, huddled round her at the bottom of the stairs – although Lily looked a bit confused and was

clutching her bags nervously. Chloe could hear them talking about Lily's mother as she went past. Maybe they were impressed by her being an actress? One of the girls was amazing-looking, with hair as long as Lily's own, but a real golden blonde. She kept tossing it around as she spoke. Chloe decided to try and catch up with Lily later instead, and headed on up the stairs.

Thankfully, the classroom was easy to find – all Chloe had to do was follow the noise. It sounded as though everyone else in the class had already arrived, and they were all trying to be as loud as possible. She took a deep breath, and walked through the door, trying to look confident. Chloe hadn't really thought that much about the scarier parts of starting a new school – having to make new friends, and maybe new enemies as well. For a start, she'd been really hoping that Bethany would be there. She'd liked the Chinese girl and thought they'd get on well. At her old school – which had been infants and juniors, so she'd been there since she was four – she knew everyone, and everyone

knew her. In fact, Chloe had been one of those people that everyone was desperate to be friends with. She wasn't the prettiest girl in the school, though her red hair was very striking, but she was funny and outgoing, and always had a good idea for something mad to do. It was going to be very weird starting all over again. And here at Lane's she wasn't going to be the only person who was confident and funny and talented . . .

The classroom was about half full, with boys and girls standing around, sitting at the tables, on the tables, on the windowsill. Everyone was in the Lane's uniform, but it certainly didn't make them all look the same. No one was sitting shyly in the corner, or pretending to read a book because they were too scared to talk. Chloe slung her bags down on an unoccupied table and wondered where to start. Luckily, a couple of girls sitting at the table behind hers gave her friendly smiles, so Chloe introduced herself.

'Hi – I'm Chloe. Did you two know each other

before you came?' Something about the two of them suggested that they were old friends.

One of the girls — they were both blonde, although one had short hair and the other one had plaits — said, 'Well, you could say that!'

'We're sisters,' the short-haired one added. 'Twins! I'm Carmen and this is Ella.'

'Wow! Yes, I can see it now. You sort of look alike, but not *that* much.' Chloe perched herself on the table and looked from Carmen to Ella and back again, confused. The two girls had identical features, but somehow they didn't look the same.

'We looked more like each other when we both had long hair,' Ella agreed. 'We tossed a coin for who had to have it cut off. We decided we weren't starting a new school and having people get us mixed up all the time. It gets really annoying.'

'Yeah, I lost. You can't do anything with short hair,' complained Carmen, 'it's really boring.'

'Couldn't you grow it to shoulder length?' asked Chloe interestedly. 'Then it'd still look different. And by the time your hair's that long, everyone would

know you apart anyway.'

'That's kind of what we were thinking,' Carmen nodded. 'We got into real trouble. Mum didn't want us to do it – we'd asked if one of us could have it cut and she said no way, so Ella did it for me. Then my mum had to take me to the hairdresser 'cause she said she wouldn't be seen dead with me looking like that.'

'Why did she mind so much? Did she like you looking the same? Put you in the same clothes all the time, that sort of thing?' Chloe asked, intrigued. She'd never actually met twins before.

The twins grinned at each other. 'No, it was because she knew she was going to have to tell our agent,' Ella explained. 'We get lots of parts because you can't really tell us apart. It's because of the rules on children working – we were in a film when we were two months old, because you can only have a baby working for a really short time. Most babies in films are actually twins, you know.'

'It wasn't as bad as Mum made out, anyway,' Carmen put in. 'We were leaving our agent because

we were coming here – you know, you aren't allowed to have any other representation than the Lane's agency while you're at the school.'

'Yeah, I had to stop being on my agent's books,' agreed Chloe, feeling quite glad she was able to say this. It made her feel not quite such an amateur next to the hugely experienced twins.

'Oh, have you worked before too?' asked Ella. 'What sort of stuff have you been in?'

Chloe had the sense not to exaggerate. She had a feeling the twins knew enough about show business to catch her out.

'Not nearly as much as you. I did quite a lot of modelling from when I was little. It's because of having red hair. It looks quite different and magazines like it. But I was in a TV series last year. A Jane Austen thing, and that was because of my hair as well. The casting director saw me in a magazine ad – for raisins!' Chloe giggled. She'd been teased a lot at school about that ad, which showed her with her hands in a bowl of raisins, looking blissed out. For weeks people had shoved raisins in her bag, and

boys kept offering to buy them for her in the lunch hall. She hadn't minded much though. The raisin people paid quite a lot, and Mum had let her buy a DVD player for her bedroom. Most of her work money went into an account to be saved for when she was older, but she was allowed the occasional treat.

'Ooh, nice. Did you get a cool costume?' Ella asked enthusiastically. 'I love clothes and every-thing. I was *so* relieved when it was Carmen who had to cut her hair.'

'Yeah, I had a couple of nice dresses. But you wouldn't believe how long it took them to do my hair every day. It had to be in perfect ringlets. It was so boring!'

'Tell me about it!' groaned Carmen. 'Everyone thinks show business is so glamorous, but no one knows about hours and hours being fitted for costumes –'

'And then they don't use them,' Ella put in.

'Oh, I know,' Chloe agreed.

Chloe could see the rest of the class quite well

from her table, and she'd been keeping an eye out for Bethany, really hoping that she'd be coming. Just then she spotted Bethany's distinctive black hair – now with red streaks.

'Oh – that's Bethany, I met her at the auditions,' she said to the twins in a pleased voice.

But Bethany wasn't alone. She and a pretty blonde girl were with Lily – actually, they were pretty much pushing her through the door, as she was in a real state. Her amazingly white skin was blotchy and her eyes were swollen. She looked as though she'd been crying for ages. Bethany and the other girl steered her towards a table, and sat her down.

'Wow, she looks really upset,' Chloe murmured.

'Do you think she's homesick or something?' Carmen asked, obviously finding it hard to believe that anyone wasn't over the moon about being at Lane's.

Chloe shook her head guiltily. 'I've got a horrible feeling – I saw her talking to some older girls downstairs. I think they must have been really mean to

her. I thought they were friends, or something . . .' She tailed off lamely, wishing she'd stopped at the stairs after all. She couldn't tear her eyes from Lily, still crying quietly.

Bethany and the blonde girl were trying to calm her down. 'Lily, honestly, they were just jealous cows,' Bethany said firmly. 'You can't let people like that get to you. I bet that Lizabeth girl is mean to everyone.'

'Yeah, we need to keep an eye on her, definitely,' the blonde girl agreed.

'Sara's right. People like that just pick on who-ever's nearest!' Bethany put an arm round Lily's trembling shoulders.

Lily took a deep breath, obviously trying to get a hold of herself. 'But the awful thing is, they're right,' she whispered. And Chloe and the twins couldn't help leaning a little closer to catch what she said.

'How come?' Sara asked, frowning.

'Well,' Lily gulped, 'they said I'd obviously only got in because of my mum, and it's true! She wrote a letter with my application form, reminding them

who I was, and how she'd been one of Lane's most successful ever students, and all sorts of stuff like that. She said there was no way they'd ever turn me down once they read it. The audition was just a formality.' She sniffed miserably.

Sara and Bethany exchanged glances over Lily's head. Then Sara took a deep breath. 'I'm sorry to be rude about your mum, Lily, but I think she's mad!'

Lily looked up, her dark brown eyes wide with surprise, but Bethany was nodding in agreement. 'I don't think they'd ever take someone just because of who their mum is. You saw the other people at your audition, didn't you? Do you seriously think you didn't deserve to get in?'

Lily shrugged. 'My dancing's not very good – I mean, it's OK, but it's nothing special. Everyone else was way better than me.'

'Well then, it must have been your acting that impressed them,' Bethany said decidedly. 'It says all over the place in the prospectus that Lane's concentrates on dancing, singing *and* acting. So acting's your thing – that doesn't mean you shouldn't be

here just as much as everybody else.'

By this time, Chloe and the twins were practically horizontal, they were leaning over so far, and Sara suddenly noticed. She stood up and folded her arms. 'Ahem. Were we saying something interesting?' she asked sweetly.

The twins pretended to be staring at something on the other side of the classroom, and Chloe flushed scarlet. 'I'm – I'm sorry,' she muttered. 'It's just – I saw you with those girls downstairs, Lily. I didn't realise –'

'You saw them picking on her, and you didn't do anything!' Sara interrupted disgustedly, and Chloe saw Bethany looking at her in disappointment, obviously remembering her from the auditions.

'It wasn't like that!' Chloe gasped.

'Yeah, right,' snapped Sara. 'First you leave those Year Eights to torture Lily, and now you can't resist sticking your big nose in where it's not wanted. Well, thank you so much for your *interest*, but this is a private conversation, if you don't mind.' And she swung back round and sat down, with her back very

meaningfully pointed at Chloe.

Bethany glared at Chloe, and turned round as well, and Chloe was left gaping. She couldn't believe what had just happened. OK, so she realised now that she should have stopped to check Lily was all right, and yes, maybe she shouldn't have been listening like that – but she hadn't meant to hurt anyone! Now she'd not only upset Bethany, who she'd really hoped would be her friend, but two other girls in her class hated her too!

Chapter Four

GINGERS TOGETHER

Red-faced, Chloe turned back to the twins, who were looking equally embarrassed.

Ella made a sympathetic face. 'I don't think she needed to be quite that mean about it,' she commented. 'And sorry, we were listening too.'

Carmen nodded apologetically. 'I should think half the class was, to be honest.'

'It doesn't matter.' Chloe smiled, though she felt

awful. She couldn't bear to think that she'd lost out on being friends with Bethany over something so stupid. She'd liked the Chinese girl so much at their audition. She told herself it didn't matter, that there were loads of other people to make friends with, but inside she felt really disappointed. She could hear Sara, Lily and Bethany muttering to each other about how nosy she was, and even though she was pretty thick-skinned, it was very hard not to feel hurt.

Just then someone dumped their bag on the table next to Chloe, startling her out of her dark thoughts. 'Hi! Do you mind if I sit here for the moment? All the other tables are full.' Chloe looked round – the classroom had filled up during her spat with Sara. But there *were* quite a few other spaces, something the owner of the bag seemed to be ignoring. Still, she wasn't going to complain, particularly as the bag belonged to a very good-looking boy, with dark blue eyes, and hair as red as her own.

He grinned at her. 'Don't you think us gingers should stick together?'

'Sure. Less of the ginger though, if you don't mind.' Chloe noted that Carmen and Ella were looking quite jealous, and cheered up slightly. 'I'm Chloe. What's your name — or do you prefer just being called Ginger? 'Cause that would be no problem. Would it?' she asked the twins, smirking. 'This is Carmen and Ella, by the way,' she added.

'Hey.' The boy nodded to the twins, and then turned back to Chloe. 'Sam Porter. I got called Ginger all the time at my last school, and I'm going to kill anyone who starts it up here. I guess no one dares mention your hair then?'

'Not if they know what's good for them.' Chloe chuckled, and cracked her knuckles threateningly. 'I have my methods . . .'

'That must be our form tutor,' murmured Ella, who was looking at the door.

A smartly dressed woman lugging a load of books had just struggled through the door. She dumped the books on her desk and smiled round the class. Most people had noticed her and were watching interestedly, but some were still deep in conversation.

'OK! Everyone sit down please! Find a seat somewhere, don't worry, you can change around later.'

They slid into seats without too much fuss, keen to find out what their timetable was like.

'I'm Miss James, your form tutor, and I'll also be teaching you maths.' She grinned as she heard the low moan that ran round the room. 'Sorry, but we do have to do the other stuff at Lane's, as well as all your dancing and drama. In fact, I'll give you a quick rundown on how it all works as soon as I've taken the register. I know you've all signed in downstairs, but it gives me a chance to put names to faces.' She went through the list on her little computer, pausing to smile as everyone answered. Her smile faded slightly when she got to Lily Ferrars, seeing her red eyes, but she didn't say anything. It was clear that Bethany and Sara were looking after her, anyway, squashed protectively on either side.

'Right, so you're all here. That's good. You've probably already realised that the school's a bit of a rabbit warren – first years have been known to disappear for days.' She paused as a few people

laughed uncertainly. 'Seriously though, because the building's been extended and modernised quite a few times, it can be hard to find your way around. Have you all got your maps?' Maps were rustled and waved at her. 'Hold on to them. By the end of the week you'll probably be fine, but the next few days you'll need them. Staff will be understanding if you're late, so don't worry.

'Let's talk about your timetable then. Can you take one of these each and pass them on, please.' She handed a sheaf of papers to Chloe and Sam, smiling as she saw the two redheads together. 'You'll see when you get them that we have academic classes in the morning, and other classes in the afternoon. I want to say now that we do expect you to work at the academic classes. However brilliant a dancer or actor you are, you won't get away with anything but working to your full potential.'

Chloe made a face. She was reasonably good at school, but she had been hoping not to have to bother too much with things like maths any more. It sounded like that wasn't an option.

47

Miss James went through the timetable, explaining how it worked and what all the different bits meant – the teacher, where the class was, that kind of thing. It took ages, and Chloe began to feel like the chances of her being in the right place at the right time with the right clothes on any day before half-term were pretty slim.

Sam noticed her worried face and nudged her.

'Don't panic. We can always ask someone.'

'I suppose so,' Chloe muttered, thinking with a wince that first you had to find someone trustworthy to ask – she could just imagine that blonde Lizabeth delighting in sending first years to the wrong place. She noticed Miss James keeping an eye on her and Sam chatting, and wondered if she was strict. She shook her red curls irritably. Just their luck to get a strict form tutor. The showdown with Sara had left her feeling as though life wasn't fair, and she was in a mood where she wanted things to complain about.

'You'll see that most of your dance classes are boys and girls separately, because the teaching style can be quite different, especially for ballet. And

thirty's quite a large class for dance, so it makes sense to split you up.'

'Typical school,' Sam agreed, pulling a ridiculous face and making Chloe laugh out loud. Miss James looked at them sharply, but didn't say anything. Chloe shrugged to herself. Right now, she didn't care what her form tutor thought of her. The long explanations droned on, and Chloe doodled on her pencil case, occasionally glancing over at the front table where Bethany, Lily and Sara were sitting. Eventually, a bell rang and Miss James smiled.

'Well, if you look at your timetable, you'll see that you have a break now. It's twenty minutes, so I'll see you back here then, and we'll start giving out your books.'

'Wow, she makes it sound like a real treat,' Chloe muttered too loudly to Sam, making him snort with laughter, and getting a very thoughtful look from Miss James.

She's beginning to think two redheads together could be dangerous, Chloe realised, chuckling to herself.

'You can go outside, or there's the cafeteria. Take your maps so you can find your way back!' Miss James called over the noise of the whole class making for the door.

Chloe headed for the cafeteria with Carmen and Ella. Sam came too, but sat with a group of boys, occasionally glancing over at Chloe's table and smirking.

'I think he really likes you,' Carmen said enviously.

'I've only known him about an hour!' Chloe protested. 'Anyway, I've got a feeling he mostly likes me because I was being rude about Miss James, that's all. I think he's a bit of a troublemaker.'

'And you're not?' Ella asked, grinning. Chloe gave her a shocked look, and Ella added quickly, 'Oh, in the nicest possible way, of course . . . But you definitely got Miss James's back up – and we've only been here one morning! That's fast work!'

Chloe frowned. She hadn't really meant to get herself a reputation. She'd seen Miss James eyeing her, but Ella had to be exaggerating, surely? As the

bell for the end of break went, Chloe vowed to be an angel for the rest of the morning. It wasn't hard — after all, putting on an act was what she was best at, that was why she was here! But she wasn't sure that Miss James bought it — her form teacher's eye seemed to be on her quite a lot of the time.

At least the second half of the morning was a bit more interesting, as they got a tour of the school. Seeing all the dance studios and practice rooms was so exciting — and the polished, empty floors seemed to call to Chloe. Knowing that every afternoon was dance, singing, drama — all her favourite things — reinforced her angel act. The argument with Sara seemed less important now, and Miss James started to look a little less suspicious.

Chloe spent lunch gossiping with the twins, and trying to work out whether she'd seen any of the films they'd been in. It was fun, and she really liked the way they never showed off about all their acting experience. Still, she supposed a lot of people at Lane's had worked already — she wouldn't be able to

51

impress many people here with one TV appearance. Chloe was really glad she'd met Carmen and Ella, but she had a feeling it might be hard to become really close friends with them, as they already had built-in best friends.

Carmen stuffed a massive forkful of tuna salad into her mouth – they'd already noticed that the cafeteria food was much healthier than at their previous schools, chips only once a week, and loads of salad options. She stabbed a finger at her timetable, and mumbled something. Ella and Chloe stared at her questioningly.

'Sorry! I said, it's tap first thing this afternoon! I'm really looking forward to it. We've hardly done any tap, have we, Ells? They said at the audition that if we got in we'd have to catch up. Have you done much before, Chloe?'

Chloe didn't want to boast, but she had – she wasn't as far on with tap as she was with ballet, but she loved it. 'Quite a bit,' she said slowly. 'I learned tap and ballet at the same dance school, and I love both. They're so different though – I'm glad it's tap

this afternoon, I feel like I need something really fun and exciting after sitting still all morning.'

'Yeah, I know what you mean,' Ella agreed. She leaned over Carmen's timetable. 'And they really pack the morning, don't they? Look, five different classes! I suppose it's to get in all the stuff we need to do.'

The other two nodded, sighing. 'And Miss James sounded as though she really meant it about having to work at normal school stuff too,' added Chloe sadly. Then she grinned. 'Still, maybe we can liven it up a bit. Hey, are we supposed to be changed for tap before the end of lunch? 'Cause if we are, we've got about three minutes!'

The twins squawked, and rushed to clear their plates away, and they all made a dash for the changing rooms, which were already full of girls trying to make sure they were in the right dance clothes. The school was really strict about wearing proper uniform – even hair had to be done the right way for classes! It was to get the students used to creating a professional impression, Chloe remembered the

prospectus saying. Chloe spotted Lily, Sara and Bethany in one corner, already nearly changed. She smiled hopefully when Bethany caught her eye, and Bethany hesitated, but then turned away. Chloe shrugged to herself. Who cared? If Bethany wanted to be like that, then that was fine by her!

Chloe and the twins were among the last to get to the studio for the tap class, but they made it. Everyone was gathered up at one end of the room, giggling nervously. This was their first real class — the first chance to show off what they could do. Chloe almost envied the twins. At least hardly knowing any tap they didn't have much to live up to!

At last two teachers arrived — Ms Driver, who Chloe had seen as she arrived in the morning, and a pianist. Ms Driver introduced herself. She was pretty and bubbly, with black hair in a knot on top of her head, and she was wearing footless tights and a Lane's T-shirt, like all the girls were. But she also had very cool red tap shoes.

Ms Driver asked for the twins, and put them in

the front row, as she'd obviously been told they hadn't done tap before. She was very nice about it though.

'Don't worry, I just want you close so I can help out if you need it,' she reassured them, and the twins nodded, flushing pink at being singled out in front of everyone. 'I think the rest of you are about the same level for tap, girls, so we'll start with a fairly basic warm-up, and then see how you get on with a simple routine.'

Ms Driver nodded to the pianist, who started to play some jazzy music. Then she led them through some stretches and moves. It was all pretty simple, and Chloe relaxed into it, enjoying stretching out her tense muscles. The stresses of the morning seemed to melt away. By the time Ms Driver demonstrated the sequence she wanted them to copy, Chloe was really enjoying herself – and she couldn't help a tiny grin as she saw Carmen and Ella looking panicked at how fast the teacher's feet moved.

She managed to catch Carmen's eye, and mouthed, 'Don't panic!' at her. Carmen grimaced.

Chloe watched the demonstration carefully, appreciating how good Ms Driver was – better than her old teacher, she thought. Still, that wasn't surprising. When it was their turn, she really went for it. Ms Driver was walking round calling out the steps, and occasionally correcting the girls' footwork. When they'd gone through it twice, she called a halt.

'That was mostly very good, girls. Obviously everyone's a bit rusty after the holidays, but nice, very nice. Well done, Carmen and Ella, I know you feel like you've got two left feet, but you'll catch up in no time with a bit of extra help.' She looked round all the girls, smiling. 'Oh, just one thing.' She beckoned to Chloe. 'Could you come here a minute?'

Chloe looked uncertainly behind her, and Ms Driver laughed.

'No, I do mean you. Just come here a minute.'

Chloe knew she'd danced really well, and she couldn't help smiling. Was Ms Driver going to ask her to demonstrate the routine to the others? Her

old tap teacher had quite often got her to do that. She threaded her way to the front, trying not to look smug.

'Mmm. Yes, I thought so. You're Chloe, aren't you? Try to remember, please, girls, that we're really strict about dress and hair at Lane's. I know it seems stupid, but you will get used to it, I promise. Next class, Chloe, can you make sure that you've got your hair straight back, and only black bands, please.'

Ms Driver was smiling and didn't sound cross, but Chloe gasped. She'd been so sure that she was about to be praised for her dancing that even this friendly criticism was a huge shock. She was wearing her hair loosely gathered in the pink scrunchie she'd always worn for tap at her old classes. It was such a silly rule! Chloe blushed furiously, then she made her big mistake.

'I don't see why we only have to wear black,' she said, glaring at the teacher.

'Perhaps not, but I'm afraid those are the rules.' Ms Driver's voice was still pleasant, but she wasn't smiling any more.

Chloe turned and marched back to her place, her shoes tapping furiously. 'How stupid can you get!' she hissed to Carmen and Ella as she passed them.

'If you don't want to be in this class, Chloe, that's fine.' Ms Driver's voice wasn't loud, but it was steely. 'Leave the class, please. When you've managed to get your head round the school dress code, perhaps you can come back. I don't have time to deal with you now.' She turned back to the pianist and asked for the music again, as though nothing had happened.

Chloe was left gulping. She didn't want to go! She hadn't meant for this to happen at all – in her dream version of this class, everyone saw what a fabulous dancer she was, and she was the girl all the others wanted to be! She didn't get sent out like a naughty five-year-old! Trying not to let anyone see her face, and trying desperately not to let her tap shoes make any noise, she scurried out of the studio.

Chapter Five

UNPLEASANT TRUTHS

Chloe was furious at being so shown up in the tap class, but she was equally determined not to show it. She made sure that when the rest of the class raced back to the changing room she was sitting tear-free and already changed on one of the benches, reading a magazine that someone had left around.

The others gave her curious glances, obviously desperate to ask her about it all, but not quite

daring. The twins bounced in last, as Ms Driver had kept them behind to talk about extra practice. They had no such qualms about not asking.

'Chloe! Are you OK? I couldn't believe you argued, I don't know whether you're mad or brave or both,' Ella giggled.

'Definitely mad,' someone muttered from behind Chloe, and she swung round to catch Sara's eye.

'I don't know how you dared, on the first day,' a dark-haired girl put in. 'But I thought it was a bit mean of her to pick on you in front of everyone. She could have just told you afterwards.'

Chloe smiled, glad of the support, then she shrugged, trying hard not to look bothered. 'Who cares, anyway?' she said lightly. 'Bet I didn't miss much. And if they're going to be like that about something as stupid as *hairbands* – well, maybe someone needs to lighten things up around here.'

'What do you mean?' Bethany put in, from the other side of the changing room, where she was struggling to get out of her tights without falling

over. 'You're not going to do something stupid, are you?'

Chloe didn't know whether to be glad that Bethany was finally talking to her, or annoyed at her critical tone. But Sara's comment had reminded her of that morning's scene all over again, and she couldn't hold back an angry answer. 'What's it to you?' she snapped, and Bethany's eyes widened.

'Nothing – I just think it would be stupid to get yourself into trouble so quickly, that's all,' she replied calmly.

Sara giggled. 'That should fit with what we've seen of her so far then,' she said, exchanging glances with Lily and Bethany.

Bethany shrugged. She seemed not to want to get into a fight – she looked as though she wished she'd never said anything. 'We all need to get changed,' she said hurriedly, turning to search through her locker.

Chloe watched her angrily. She was miserable enough to want to get in a real row with someone, but deep down – too deep for her to admit it right

now – she still wished she and Bethany could be friends.

It was hard for Chloe to go home and pretend that everything was OK. It would have been so nice to talk to her mum and ask for her advice, but Chloe didn't want to burst her bubble. Her mum had flung open the door as she saw her coming down the path, and raced out to meet her, wanting to hear all about it. Then she had to go through it all again when her dad got home. The worst thing was that telling them about her fabulous new school was one of the things Chloe had been really looking forward to. She managed to make a good story of it anyway, and was fairly sure she had been completely convincing. Chloe cried herself to sleep that night, desperately disappointed, and wondering just how it had all gone so wrong.

The next morning, she woke up feeling determined – she wasn't going to let anyone at school see that she wasn't happy. Least of all Bethany and her little gang. She marched through the glass doors,

and was met almost immediately in the corridor by Sam and a group of boys.

'Hey, Chloe! Heard you had a fun time in tap yesterday!' Sam pretended to examine her hair. 'Hmm, I hope that's a uniform hairband, young lady . . .'

He was grinning, but not in a mean way, and Chloe grinned back. 'Funny. I hadn't got you down as someone who was interested in hair accessories, Sam. If only I'd known. I've got some cute Hello Kitty clips at home, they'd really bring out your ginger highlights.'

Sam's look of horror was great, and the other boys fell about laughing while Chloe pretended to hunt through her bag for hairbands for him. She stayed chatting to the boys until the bell went, mostly complaining about how awful their timetable was, and hearing horror stories about the boys' tap teacher, who was apparently a real perfectionist. They all piled into their classroom late, and Miss James gave Chloe and Sam a look that seemed to say she wasn't surprised . . .

Chloe had never exactly been a teacher's pet, but

the teachers at her last school had at least liked her. Chloe had a feeling that Ms Driver had probably told Miss James about the argument in tap. It felt really weird being someone who was expected to get into trouble. Chloe wasn't sure whether she should behave perfectly so as to make up for yesterday, or just go with it. If everyone thought she was difficult – even Carmen and Ella seemed to think so, and it had certainly made her popular with Sam and the other boys – then maybe she should try to live up to her new reputation?

Proper classes started that morning, and Chloe sat with Carmen and Ella and Sam's group of mates. Was it Chloe's imagination, or did all the teachers keep a careful eye on them? By the time both the history and English teachers had told them all off for talking and giggling – when Chloe was sure they weren't worse than anyone else – Chloe was starting to feel picked on.

The rest of the first week seemed to go really quickly. It was odd – nothing was quite as Chloe had

imagined, and sometimes she wished she had more good friends at Lane's to talk it all over with. She'd been right about Carmen and Ella. The twins were great fun, and they'd invited her to come over to their house one night, which she was really pleased about, but they were so much each other's best friends that there wasn't much room for anyone else. Chloe had Sam and the boys to chat to as well, but there was no way she was opening her heart to them!

At least she seemed to have made it up with Ms Driver. For their next tap class, on Thursday, she made sure she was perfectly dressed, and followed all the instructions as carefully as she could. No silly mistakes. Ms Driver actually told her that her foot-work was very neat, and gave her a huge smile when she completed a routine perfectly. So that was good – Chloe might like being a bit cheeky in morning classes, but she loved tap, and she didn't want the classes spoilt by a teacher who couldn't stand her.

Ballet was great too – Miss Jasper's methods were different from her old ballet school, but she was a

really good teacher, and Chloe felt so supple and stretched out after her class that she just wanted to lie down on the changing-room floor and have a nap!

By the weekend, Chloe was so tired that she felt like spending the whole two days in bed. She'd had no idea what hard work stage school would be. Lying in bed late on Sunday morning, gazing at her *Chicago* poster (she was definitely going to be in that one day!), Chloe wondered if it would get any easier. It wasn't that she wished she was at the local secondary school, like Sophie – no way! But . . . Oh, she didn't know what . . . She supposed she'd had this fairy-tale idea that if only she could get into Lane's, everything would be happy ever after. And it just wasn't quite working out like that.

Dashing through the corridors to French the next Tuesday, she saw Mr Townsend, their history teacher, talking quietly to someone. Obviously he had no idea who was behind him.

'Year Seven are a nightmare, aren't they?

I wouldn't have thought they could get worse than last year's lot, but they've managed it. That red-haired girl, Chloe. She's got half the class thinking she's hilarious, and she just doesn't shut up. It only takes the one.' He sighed.

'Oh, I know.' The dark-haired woman, their French teacher Ms LeBrun, grimaced. 'You normally hope they might behave for at least the first couple of weeks – *and* I've got a double with them.' Her French accent was very pretty, but Chloe was too furious to appreciate it. She hadn't even done any-thing in history lessons, just told Carmen and Ella a couple of jokes. How unfair was that?

Needless to say, Chloe was not at her best in French. She was seething. Once in the classroom, she gazed at the board, not seeing it at all. If that was what the Lane's staff thought of her, then fine! She would really give them something to think about.

'Chloe!' Ms LeBrun's soft voice had an edge to it now. 'Listen, please! *Quel âge as-tu?*'

Chloe gaped at her. She had absolutely no idea

what the French teacher was talking about.

'*Onze!*' Sam hissed at her out of the corner of his mouth. 'It's *onze* for eleven, go on!'

Unfortunately, since Chloe hadn't heard a word Ms LeBrun had said since the start of the lesson, she didn't even understand what Sam was trying to tell her. On what? She just blinked at the teacher, looking confused.

'Fine. Chloe, you'll be doing extra homework, see me about it at the end. Sam, seeing as you seem able to tell Chloe what she ought to be saying, perhaps you'd like to answer instead.'

Sam coughed, looking embarrassed. 'Er, *j'ai onze ans.*'

At the end of the class, Chloe slunk sulkily up to Ms LeBrun's desk. She knew it was her own fault for not listening, but it didn't make it any easier. Yet another telling off, plus a whole extra exercise to do from their textbook, didn't make her feel like behaving at all. Quite the opposite, in fact. She felt more like she was going to explode. She had Carmen and Ella, and a couple of the other girls from her class,

choking on their lunch with her imitation of Ms LeBrun forgetting how to speak English because she was so furious with Chloe. She was still bubbling over in ballet, and for once, the exercises at the barre didn't have their usual magic effect.

Miss Jasper had arranged them at the barre, so Bethany was behind Chloe, and Carmen and Ella were at the other end of the line. But Chloe just had to have someone as an audience, so Bethany would have to do. Miss Jasper was watching the girls at the other end as they did their *pliés*, trying to get Lily to bend deeper. Chloe started to exaggerate her movements, waggling her bottom like a duck as she sank into the bend. She heard a stifled snigger from behind her, and grinned to herself. Bethany had seen. As she came up again she twitched her neck like a bird pecking – and then she did it all again, adding a little flap with the hand that wasn't on the barre, turning out her feet, making a tiny little hissy quack noise. By the fourth time, Bethany just couldn't cope. She burst out laughing, and Miss Jasper turned round sharply – or as sharply as their

super-graceful ballet teacher ever moved.

'Who was that? Bethany! What's so funny about *pliés*? You girls are supposed to be concentrating!'

Chloe sneaked a quick look over her shoulder. Bethany was scarlet, and she glared back at her. Chloe widened her eyes apologetically. She'd meant to make Bethany laugh, but she hadn't really thought that she'd get into trouble. She wondered if she ought to tell Miss Jasper that it was her fault.

'I'm sorry,' Bethany whispered. 'I didn't mean to laugh.'

'Then stop disrupting my class. Girls! Did I tell the rest of you to stop?'

Everyone had been peering round to see what was going on, and now they suddenly snapped back into their positions, trying to look as though they'd never moved.

'And one! And two!' Miss Jasper sounded really annoyed, and Chloe's silly mood vanished. Poor Bethany!

At the end of the class, Bethany shot out of the

studio as soon as it was obvious that Miss Jasper wasn't going to have another go about her laughing. Chloe raced after her, still struggling with her fleece. She really wanted to apologise.

Bethany was in the changing room, slamming her locker door and looking really cross.

'I'm really sorry! I didn't mean to get you into trouble,' Chloe panted out.

'Yeah, right! Of course you did. You made me laugh on purpose!' Bethany was practically spitting.

'Well, yeah, I meant to make you laugh, but I didn't know she'd have a go at you! I really am sorry.'

'I don't care if you're sorry or not! You totally spoilt that class for me, and now she's going to be watching me like a hawk for ages. Why do you have to be so stupid and . . . and childish, Chloe! Why can't you just grow up?'

Chloe frowned. 'Hey, it was only a joke. Don't take it so seriously!'

'She has to take it seriously, stupid. *She* was the one who got into trouble!' The rest of the class were back now, and Sara was looking almost as angry as

her friend. 'I didn't notice you telling Miss Jasper it was all your fault!'

'Mind your own business!' Chloe snapped.

'Bethany's my friend, so it is my business – which you might understand if you had any real friends, Chloe, instead of just an audience all the time.'

Chloe gasped. Was that really what they all thought of her? She looked quickly round the group of girls, and saw that quite a few of them were nodding. Carmen and Ella caught her eye, and looked away quickly. Chloe could feel the tears welling up, but she wasn't going to give Bethany and Sara the satisfaction of knowing they'd made her cry.

'You think *I'm* childish! If you weren't such a total baby, you'd know how to take a joke,' she snarled at Bethany. Then she stalked across the changing room to grab her stuff for a shower. She didn't care if she was late for their drama improvisation. She needed some alone-time.

Chloe was far too proud to admit that Bethany and Sara's comments had got to her – to anyone but

herself, that is. The looks on the other girls' faces had suddenly made her realise that she was wasting the best opportunity she'd ever been given. The odd joke every so often was OK – she wasn't aiming to be a saint. But so far, she'd got totally on the wrong side of her form tutor, and several of the other academic staff (and it was bound to show up on her end-of-term report, she thought worriedly). She'd annoyed her tap teacher, and messed around in ballet and got someone else in trouble.

As she stomped grimly along to the tube station that afternoon, she tried to be honest with herself. Sam was nice, but he and his mates liked her because she was 'fun' – which meant she fooled around and livened up boring lessons for them. Would they even want to hang around with her if she behaved? She wasn't sure, and it was really embarrassing to think like that about herself. As if she had to do tricks all the time to be noticed, like a performing dog! She was pretty sure Carmen and Ella did like her. In fact, might they like her even more if she wasn't trying to impress everyone the

whole time? They were so sensible and down to earth.

She felt her nose start to run again (just her luck to be someone who couldn't cry romantically) and she sniffed furiously. While she was being honest, she might as well do it properly and admit that she was really jealous of Bethany, Lily and Sara. She so wished she had someone who'd stick up for her like Sara had for Bethany that afternoon! They were always together, and they seemed to have fun without having to try so hard.

By the time she opened her front door, Chloe felt exhausted with the double effort of thinking and trying not to cry. She dropped her bag in the hall and trailed into the kitchen. Her mum only worked part-time, so she was around when Chloe got home from school. Chloe had been saying for ages that she was perfectly capable of making her own tea, but for once, she was really glad her mum was there. She was cooking, and called out without looking round.

'Hi sweetheart, I'll be with you in a minute.'

Chloe nodded, and then realised her mum couldn't see her. She wandered over to lean against the counter, and her mum smiled round at her.

'Good day?'

Chloe gave a funny little laugh, and then started to cry. She couldn't help it. She put her arms round her mum's waist, and gave her a hug.

'Hey! What's wrong?' Mrs Ford abandoned her pasta sauce to hug Chloe back.

'Nothing. I just had a really horrible day. Had a fight with somebody,' Chloe snuffled into her mum's sweater.

'Oh, Chlo, everyone has days like that some-times. Do you think you can make it up?'

'I don't know. It doesn't matter though, I know what I'm going to do.' This was true. Chloe had worked out a plan – it wasn't something she was exactly looking forward to, but the new-look Chloe Ford would be going back to Lane's the next day.

Everyone noticed that Chloe was quieter than usual the next morning. She sat with Carmen and Ella,

which was what she normally did, but she didn't giggle and chat her way through double science. She just listened, even though Mrs Taylor was droning on and on about different ways heat could move through substances – or something like that. Halfway through, Sam chucked a note across one of the benches at her, but it missed, and even though she could have pretended to drop a pen or something to get it, she just gave him an apologetic look, and went back to gazing at the board.

At lunch she disappeared to the cafeteria before the others had got their stuff together, bought a sandwich, and then set off down a little staircase by the drama studios to put her plan into action. Lane's had loads of practice rooms in the basement – all sizes. They were meant for music practice, and the outside staff who came to teach extra music lessons used them. Sometimes groups of students would rehearse in them. But basically, anyone who wanted could use them, and hardly anyone bothered with the booking system. You just turned up and looked for one that was free.

Armed with a book of songs from the musicals that she'd got from the library at morning break, Chloe sneaked along the corridor, peering though the glass panels, and eventually found a cubbyhole with a piano and just about enough room to open the door and squeeze in. It was perfect. The best thing was that although she was keen on singing, she hadn't exactly been up for extra work before now, so no one was likely to look for her here. She heaved a sigh of relief, and settled herself in front of the piano, flicking through the book for something she felt like. Then she giggled. 'My Favourite Things' from *The Sound of Music*. That was about right – thinking about her favourite things (glitter lipgloss and chocolate buttons) would definitely cheer her up right now, even if warm woollen mittens didn't really do it for her. Chloe wasn't brilliant at the piano, but she knew enough to pick out a tune she wanted to sing, and it was something she often did on her keyboard at home. She practised the voice exercises they'd been doing in singing too – she knew she really needed to work on her projection,

especially if she wanted to be in musicals someday. Power was really important. She was actually surprised how quickly the lunch break went, and she had to cram in her sandwich at the last minute.

People had noticed she wasn't around though. Sam tackled her about it at afternoon registration.

'Hey, where were you? I looked for you at lunch. Tom and Jake were having a spaghetti fight, you missed it.'

Chloe dithered. She couldn't tell Sam that he was a bad influence and she was avoiding him. It would make her sound totally sad, and anyway, she still really liked him – she just didn't want to be hanging round with his mates getting into trouble. Although she did wish she'd seen Tom and Jake covered in spaghetti.

'Extra music practice,' she said slowly, hoping that it sounded like something official, rather than hiding in a music room on her own . . .

'Oh, OK.' Sam shrugged.

Chloe breathed a sigh of relief. She seemed to have got away with it. But Carmen and Ella were

giving her a scarily identical thoughtful look, and as Sam wandered back to his mates across the classroom, Ella asked, 'Since when do you have extra practice? I mean, we've been having all those extra lunchtime tap classes with Ms Driver, but you're not behind in anything.'

'Um. My mum wants me to keep up with piano, that's all,' Chloe muttered. It was actually true – Chloe's mum was always saying she ought to have more lessons. She wished she could tell Carmen and Ella what was really going on, but she was still feeling fragile after the fight yesterday. She didn't know the twins well enough to admit that she was feeling friendless and lonely, and she was spending all her lunchtimes on her own! She had a horrible feeling they'd think her big decision to be 'good' was really funny . . .

Chapter Six

UNDER SUSPICION

The times for the next set of LAMDA acting exams were announced on Monday – everyone at school had known they were coming up, but knowing exactly when they were happening threw all the candidates into a panic. External exams like LAMDA were a really serious thing at Lane's, and everyone was expected to do well. None of the Year Sevens were entering of course, but suddenly everywhere

they went was full of older students rehearsing and stressing, and generally being a total pain.

It got worse all week, until even Chloe's favourite tiny little practice room got nicked on the Friday. Chloe was happily playing around with a couple of songs from *West Side Story*, when a couple of Year Nines barged in.

'What are *you* doing in here?' one of the girls asked Chloe, as though she'd just found a small bug in her lunch.

Chloe had been mid-song, and she wasn't happy about being interrupted. Besides, she knew no one else had booked the room. 'Duh, practising,' she snapped. 'It *is* a practice room.'

'Well, get out. We need to be in here,' the older girl ordered.

Chloe swung round on the piano stool and folded her arms. 'Why should I? You didn't book the room, there's no name on the door. I've got just as much right to be here as you have.'

'We've got exams,' the other girl started to explain, in a more friendly sort of way. 'We really

need to practise.'

'Yeah, I can tell,' muttered Chloe. 'Not sure it's worth you bothering though.' She grabbed her music and stomped out, seething.

She wasn't the only one. Carmen and Ella had been practising tap in one of the other rooms – they were desperate to catch up with the rest of the class, and they were furious at being chucked out. They greeted Chloe sympathetically as she stormed into their form room, and the three of them spent the rest of lunch moaning about uppity seniors.

'Somebody ought to teach them they don't own the school,' Chloe grumbled, as they all walked into the studio for their drama class.

'Someone *should*,' Carmen agreed, slinging her bag down. 'But we can't, can we? And none of the staff are going to be on our side.'

'No, they just say it's a very important time, and so on, and so on,' complained Chloe loudly. 'It's so unfair. We should do something ourselves to pay them back.'

'That sounds very dramatic, Chloe,' their acting

teacher commented as he walked in. 'Hope you're not talking about anyone in the staff room.'

'Mr Lessing, everyone keeps chucking us out of the practice rooms,' Ella complained.

'Oh, I see. Well, the thing is, with the exams coming up, it's a very important time for some of the older students right now . . .' Mr Lessing said vaguely. He was getting stuff out of his bag, so he didn't see the look Carmen, Ella, Chloe and the others exchanged – which was probably just as well. He finally managed to find what he'd been rooting about in his bag for, and turned back round flourishing it, by which time they were more interested in why he was waving an umbrella about like a lunatic than moaning about practice rooms.

'*This* is today's theme!' he announced dramatically.

'An umbrella?' It was Jake, Sam's friend, and he sounded as though he thought Mr Lessing might have lost it entirely.

'Yes, well spotted, Jake. Can't get anything past you, can I? Spread yourselves out round the room.

Today's lesson is pass the umbrella.' Mr Lessing was grinning at them all. 'Not as stupid as it sounds. I want to see as many different ways to pass the umbrella as you can think of. Are you going to be Gene Kelly singing in the rain –' here he performed a short solo dance number, which was dreadful – 'you remember he gives the umbrella to a passer-by – or are you going to be a spy stabbing someone with the poisoned tip? You can talk, mime, whatever you want, and the umbrella doesn't always have to *be* an umbrella, if you see what I mean. I want to see what you come up with, and I'm just going to watch.'

The class brightened up. OK, so it was a mad idea, but it was a *good* mad idea. Acting classes so far had been fine, but nothing really exciting. Chloe happened to catch Lily's eye and grinned excitedly at her. Lily grinned back, and then they both remembered they officially didn't get on, and scowled.

'Right, Lily, with that face, you definitely have to start.' Mr Lessing handed her the umbrella with a formal bow, and Lily looked panicked for a second.

Then she straightened up, and the others watched in surprise as she shook out the skirt of her school uniform as though it was a satin dress, and strolled off up the room, the umbrella open and held above her head like a parasol. None of them had really seen Lily act that much before, and it was amazing how she was suddenly, clearly, a grand lady walking in the park. She wandered idly back down the studio, and then her face changed to a look of horror. She tugged at the umbrella, and stretched up on tiptoe, as though it was pulling away from her. A sudden gust of wind had caught it. She threw it lightly up into the air, and was left looking cross and embarrassed, watching her sunshade fly off across the park. The she was back to being Lily again, waiting to see what Sam would do with the umbrella now he'd grabbed it.

'That was brilliant,' Chloe whispered to her. She didn't care that they weren't friends. She'd been so impressed, she just had to say something. Lily just shrugged and smiled, and they went back to watching.

It was a fantastic class, and Chloe was still giggling about it on her way home. She felt like she'd really seen what Lane's was about – and she loved it. She'd even got a smile off Lily! She felt on top of the world.

The LAMDA drama exams were the next Monday, and the atmosphere at school was electric. Miss James reminded her class about them while she was doing the register, but there was no way anyone could forget.

'Just be really quiet if you're passing the drama studios. Remember it could be you taking exams soon, so be considerate, please.'

Around the school everyone was mouse-like – they might have been annoyed the previous week, but practically all the Year Sevens had done some kind of drama or dance exams before. They knew how nerve-wracking it could be, and how even a noise outside could make someone forget their words – that could mean the difference between a distinction and a merit, or even a pass and a fail.

It was a relief for Chloe actually to make a noise down in her little practice room at lunchtime. She really threw herself into the *West Side Story* songs she'd picked out for today. She was concentrating hard, and it was a horrible shock when an alarm bell suddenly exploded right next to her – or that's what it felt like anyway. They hadn't had a fire practice yet, but she guessed that was what it was, so after ten seconds of staring at her music like a startled rabbit, she grabbed her stuff and headed for the courtyard, where they'd been told to assemble if the alarm went off.

The corridors were heaving with half-dressed students – it was nearly the end of lunch and people were getting ready for afternoon classes. Chloe spotted the Year Nine girl who'd been so rude to her coming down the corridor from the drama studio, looking furious – obviously she'd been in her exam, as Mr Lessing and a tall, grey-haired lady, who had to be the examiner, were just coming out of the studio too. The Year Nine girl glared at Chloe suspiciously, and Chloe quickly stuck out her

tongue – she couldn't resist. She did feel sorry for the girl though. It was terrible timing for a fire alarm.

Quite a few of the students out on the courtyard were in dance clothes and fleeces – luckily it was a fairly nice September day, not too cold. Chloe should have been getting changed for tap, but she'd lost track of time while she had been practising. Some of the ballet people were worst off, as they only had tops and tights. The rules for fire alarms were strict – grab fleece and go, no getting changed or hunting around for bags.

All the students had to line up alphabetically in year groups, which was a bit of a guessing game for the Year Sevens, as they hadn't really learned each other's surnames. Chloe found herself in between a couple of girls she didn't know all that well, so she just watched what was going on rather than chatting. The staff seemed to be dashing around everywhere, looking frazzled. Chloe had assumed this was a planned fire practice, but she started to wonder if it was a real alarm – surely if it was only a practice everyone would know what they were doing a bit more?

A group of Year Eights in the line next to her seemed to be thinking along the same lines. 'It's so stupid!' Chloe caught someone say in a very superior voice. Somehow it wasn't a surprise to find that it was Lizabeth, the blonde girl who'd upset Lily on their first morning. 'I mean, why today of all days? I know they have to have a fire practice at the beginning of term so as to get the little ones –' here she cast a disgusted glance at the line of Year Sevens, and Chloe rolled her eyes at the girl behind her – 'up to speed, but today's *so* important. My exam is meant to be in half an hour's time. I mean honestly, how am I meant to concentrate on my exam pieces? It's just not fair. I might have to appeal if I don't get a distinction. Mr Lessing absolutely *promised* me I would.' Somehow Chloe couldn't imagine Mr Lessing saying any such thing, but Lizabeth did have a point.

'But I don't think they did pick today, Lizabeth,' another Year Eight girl put in. 'I heard Miss Jasper saying that it was a total shock. She sounded really annoyed about it as well.'

'You mean there's an actual fire?' Lizabeth's voice was disbelieving.

'No-oo, I don't think so. No, she was annoyed because she said someone must have set the alarm off – on purpose.'

'Nobody would do anything that stupid,' Lizabeth said dismissively. 'They'd get roasted alive. I mean, let alone what the school would say, if I found out who it was I'd kill them!' Her pretty face was pale with anger, and Chloe shuddered. How could someone that beautiful be so scary-looking?

'Well, if it was just a practice, we'd be going back in by now,' her friend pointed out. 'It's been ages, and they've marked us all off. And look – why's Ms Purcell talking to all the staff like that? There's none of this messing about normally, it's back into school as soon as we're out. No one wants us to miss class time.'

Just as she spoke, the school principal stepped forward, and motioned for silence. Ms Purcell didn't teach many drama classes any more, she was too busy, but Chloe could see why everyone raved about them. She had so much presence.

'As many of you may have guessed, this was not a scheduled fire alarm drill.' Her beautiful voice carried easily across the courtyard. A low hum of chatter ran round the lines at her words, but she hushed it with an upraised hand. 'It seems that the fire alarm was set off deliberately — and we don't know who by. Please be certain, though, that we will be investigating. Setting off a fire alarm on a day like today, when you have all been asked to keep noise levels down out of consideration for students taking exams, is incredibly selfish and stupid. Not to mention rude to our visiting examiner. If anyone has anything to say about this, they had better to speak to their form tutor. Now, everyone back to their classes please, this silly little stunt has wasted quite enough time already.' And she swept round and led the way back into school, every inch of her radiating outrage. The staff followed her, and Chloe spotted Mr Lessing and the examiner again. He was looking very apologetic. The Year Nine girl who'd been in her exam broke out of her line and chased after them, and seemed to be telling them something

very important, if her hands were anything to go by. She was flapping about like a mad thing. Mr Lessing looked thoughtfully at Chloe as he went past the lines, and the Year Nine girl gave her another scowl, but this time she looked almost triumphant, and Chloe wondered why. She decided against sticking her tongue out again.

The school followed, class by class, everyone chattering now. Who could have done it? Who would dare? Chloe hung back to wait for Carmen and Ella, who were wearing an odd selection of school uniform and tap clothes. She was too buzzy with curiosity to notice the reserved looks that came over their faces when they saw her.

'Isn't it mad?' she giggled. 'I wonder who it was. Do you think someone panicked about their exam and smashed the fire alarm to get out of it?'

When the twins didn't answer she gave them a questioning look. 'What's up?'

Carmen shrugged, and exchanged glances with Ella. 'Well, we did wonder if it was you . . .' she admitted.

'What?' Chloe was stunned.

'You said in drama on Friday that someone ought to get those seniors back for being such pains, and – well, someone has, haven't they?'

'But it wasn't me!' Chloe gazed at the twins, horror-struck. She'd never try and deliberately ruin someone's chances in an exam . . . Even though she had said that someone should . . . Oh, help! 'It really wasn't, honestly. I mean, I know I said that, but I just meant, I don't know, hide their dance clothes or something. Not interrupt the exams!'

It was such a shock – just like the scene in the changing rooms all over again. Chloe felt really hurt that the twins thought she was the sort of person who would do that – but then they'd seen her messing around in loads of classes. She'd got Bethany into trouble, hadn't she? And then had a fight with her about it. She gulped. What if other people thought the same thing? And then Chloe felt suddenly sick as she remembered the Year Nine girl, and the odd look Mr Lessing had given her. Had that girl told him Chloe was hanging around in the

corridor? Had she told Mr Lessing it was *Chloe* who'd set off the fire alarm?

Chloe had never danced as badly as she did that day. Ms Driver gave her several questioning looks as she messed up her steps, and then eventually lost her patience. Chloe had just gone in completely the wrong direction and crashed into the rest of her line, and now half the class was glaring at her.

'Chloe, concentrate! What *is* the matter with you this afternoon?' Ms Driver snapped.

'She knows she's in big trouble,' somebody muttered from the back of the class. Chloe wasn't sure who it was. Her dancing didn't improve much, but at least she managed to go the same way as everyone else for the rest of the lesson. She skulked at the back for most of their singing class, and worriedly noticed several more curious looks from the rest of her year. Sam's friends Tom and Jake gave her admiring glances as they passed her, and Chloe felt sicker and sicker. Did *everyone* think she'd set off the fire alarm?

At final registration, Miss James was looking really grim, and Chloe just knew what was coming. When she'd finished the register, she beckoned Chloe over, and Chloe knew the rest of the class was staring at her as she trailed up to the front. Miss James was clearly trying not to look too disgusted with her, but she couldn't keep the disappointment out of her voice. 'Chloe, get your things and go down to Ms Purcell's office, please. She wants to see you.'

Chloe felt rather than heard the buzz of whispering that broke out behind her.

'It *was* her!'

'I told you!'

'Do you think she'll get expelled?'

Staring at the floor, not wanting to see the class all eyeing her suspiciously, she fetched her bag, and headed for the office. She didn't see Lily, Sara and Bethany staring worriedly after her.

Chloe stood outside the door of the office, wondering miserably what she was supposed to do now.

Did she knock, or just wait for Ms Purcell to come out? The secretary wasn't at her desk to ask. Suddenly, the door opened, nearly bumping into her, and she skipped backwards.

'Oh, Chloe, you're here.' Mr Lessing frowned down at her. 'You'd better come in.' He stood back to let her pass him, and Chloe stumbled across what seemed like acres of carpet towards Ms Purcell's desk. The principal looked thoughtfully at her.

'I imagine you know why you're here, Chloe?'

Chloe just nodded, and Ms Purcell's expression hardened. 'We really don't like stupid stunts like that here. You could have jeopardised several people's drama exams today.'

'But I didn't! Really, I was practising and I heard the bell. It wasn't me!' Chloe's voice was a panicked squeak, she was so eager to convince Ms Purcell.

'One of the exam candidates saw you hanging around, Chloe, and she seems to think you set off the alarm during her exam as some kind of revenge for an incident last week. The rest of your class doesn't seem very surprised that you were involved,

either. And Mr Lessing has just been telling me about your little outburst in his class last week – and that he also saw you up by the studios just after the alarm had been set off. You were on your own, while the rest of your year were changing for their tap class. Why was that?'

'I forgot,' Chloe muttered. It didn't sound very convincing, she realised.

'Mmmm. And you say you were practising? On your own?' Ms Purcell was watching her carefully.

'Yes. I was in one of the practice rooms, just doing some singing practice . . .' Chloe trailed off. No one was ever going to believe this!

'I have to say, Chloe, that the reports I've had of you from various members of staff don't suggest that you're the sort of person who would be practising her singing – on her own.'

Chloe blinked miserably, feeling the tears welling up, and her stupid nose starting to run again. 'I was,' she muttered. 'I can't prove it, but I was.'

Ms Purcell sighed, and exchanged a glance with Mr Lessing. 'Well, as you say, you can't prove that

you weren't setting off the fire alarm – and we can't prove that you were. I'm sorry, Chloe, but your behaviour so far this term hasn't helped you. If you say you didn't do it, I have to accept that, but please consider yourself warned. If I have any more complaints about you this term, you'll be suspended. You can go.'

By this time the tears were streaming down Chloe's face, and she made blindly for the door. Thankfully the corridors had cleared in the time the interview had taken, and only the odd person was around to stare at her as she scurried out of school. She didn't even stop to get her coat, just got away as fast as she could. Chloe wasn't sure she could ever go back.

Chapter Seven
LANE'S MOST WANTED

The next morning, the whole school seemed to know that it had been a red-haired Year Seven girl who set off the fire alarm. Chloe crept through the entrance hall feeling like a famous actress who'd been spotted having a bad hair day.

She'd spent her whole journey home the previous day making plans for changing schools, but she'd realised when she got home that there was no way

her parents would ever let her — not after just two weeks. And that was another thing — what were they going to say? How could she even start to explain?

It turned out that she didn't need to. Ms Purcell had already rung home — and Chloe's mum was furious. Not with Chloe, but with the school. From the sound of it, she'd really told Ms Purcell where to get off. Chloe wasn't sure if she was exaggerating a bit (she couldn't imagine anyone having a go at Ms Purcell), but it certainly sounded as if Mum had stuck up for her.

She met Chloe at the door, with her hair all sticking up where she'd run her fingers through it while she was on the phone. Chloe knew that look — she always thought of it as her mother's angry cat pose. 'What have you been doing, Chloe?' she demanded crossly.

'It wasn't me!' Chloe's voice was horrified. She'd been hoping to have some more time to gather her thoughts before she had to mention this to Mum and Dad. Like maybe another week or so . . .

'Oh, I know you didn't set off the fire alarm, but

that woman kept saying that you'd been misbehaving in classes. She said you hang around with a group of boys and you're a bad influence on each other. That doesn't sound like you!'

Chloe shrugged. She was beginning to feel that since starting at Lane's she'd turned into an entirely different person. She didn't know who she was any more, so why should her mum?

'Don't shrug at me like that, Chloe, this is important! I could see you were having a hard time settling in at school, but I never imagined I'd get a phone call like that about you.'

Chloe said nothing. What could she say, after all? Sorry? She *was* sorry, but that wasn't going to make everything better. She wasn't sure that anything could.

'Maybe we were wrong to let you audition for that school,' her mother said worriedly. 'You wanted it so much, but it's obviously not right for you. You might be better off at St Joe's after all.'

'No!' Chloe even startled herself. Her mum looked at her like she'd grown wings.

'It was only a thought, darling!'

'Please. Please, Mum.' She hadn't realised until her mother suggested it how much she would hate to go to school anywhere else. OK, so on the way home she'd been planning how to persuade her parents to let her leave Lane's, but now her mum seemed to be seriously thinking about it . . . Well, she just couldn't! Even if for the rest of her time at school everyone thought she was the girl who'd set off the fire alarm, she was *staying*.

Chloe scurried up the stairs to her form room, wishing she'd thought to bring a big hat. Or maybe a blanket to put over her head. Everyone she passed stared at her, and muttered to their friends. Thank goodness Lizabeth wasn't around – Chloe had seen what she could do, and she didn't fancy being in the same state as Lily had been on the first day. She kept her head down as she shot up the stairs, really not wanting to see anyone. Unfortunately this meant she entirely missed Bethany, Sara and Lily who were at the top . . .

'Ow!' Lily made a wild grab for the banister, and just managed to avoid going flying. Sara snatched her back from the top step.

'Are you mad? Look where you're going! Oh – Chloe, it's you.' Bethany's voice changed. 'Are you OK?' She picked up Chloe's bag, and put a hand on her arm. 'You look awful.'

'Cheers,' Chloe muttered crossly. Bethany was being suspiciously nice, and she didn't know how to react. Besides, no one likes being told they look terrible, even if they know it's true.

'Everyone's saying you're going to be expelled,' Bethany said worriedly.

'Oh, great,' Chloe sighed and sat down on the stairs. She suddenly felt too tired and depressed even to stand up. 'Just what I need. Why do you care anyway?' she added, looking up at the three of them. 'You hate me. You ought to be pleased.'

Bethany sat down beside her, and glared at Sara and Lily. Lily was still rubbing her arm, where Sara had grabbed her, but she sat down on the step above, and eventually Sara gave an irritated sigh and

flumped down next to her.

'We don't hate you.'

Somehow Bethany being so nice was hard for Chloe to take, and her voice wobbled as she answered. 'Well, you should. With the Lizabeth thing, and then getting you in trouble with Miss Jasper. I'd hate me.'

'Don't tempt me,' Sara said. 'I could be persuaded.'

And Bethany scowled at her. 'Sara! Stop it! Chloe's never even done anything to you. Anyway, it's not important right now. Chloe, we want to know why you haven't told Ms Purcell you didn't set the alarm off.'

'I did!' Chloe looked up at them, surprised. 'Of course I told her! But they don't believe me. They think I did it, but they can't prove it, so I'm on a warning. If I do anything else wrong all term, I'll get suspended,' she said miserably.

'Right. Well, in that case we'll have to go and see Miss James,' Bethany said decisively.

Chloe gaped at her. 'Why? Miss James really

does hate me.'

'We need to tell her it wasn't you.' Lily leaned down from the step above. 'We could go to Ms Purcell, I suppose, but I'd rather not.'

Chloe smiled at her, but she felt like crying. Why on earth did these three believe her, when no one else did?

'Even if we didn't know for sure, I don't think you'd actually have set off the alarm with the exams going on.' Lily's voice was very serious. 'Not after that drama lesson on Friday — you just wouldn't. I could see how much it meant to you, that class.'

'And anyway, we do know it wasn't you, and Bethany and Lily don't think you deserve to have everyone thinking it was.' Sara sniffed. 'Personally, I think it might do you good, but I'm outvoted.'

'But — but — how do you know?' Chloe asked, feeling totally bewildered.

'We saw you!' Bethany grinned at her. 'You were in one of the practice rooms, weren't you?'

'Yeah — but what were you doing?' Chloe could feel a little bubble of happiness lifting inside her. For

the first time since Carmen and Ella had told her their suspicions yesterday, the horrible, desperate feeling was starting to go away.

'I was going to see if I could change the time for my violin lesson. My teacher uses one of those rooms,' Sara explained. 'Lily and Bethany came with me.' She stood up. 'Come on then. If we're going to find Miss James before school starts, we'd better go now.'

It felt so different now, walking down to the staff room together with Lily, Bethany and Sara. Somehow it didn't matter that everyone was still staring. They passed Carmen and Ella just coming in, and the twins looked totally confused seeing them all together. Chloe could see they were desperately trying to work out what was going on. She gave them a quick smile, but still felt embarrassed about talking to them.

Somehow it was a bit of a shock arriving outside the staff room. It wasn't as bad as Ms Purcell's office, but Chloe really didn't feel like knocking. She looked hopefully at Bethany.

'Oh, all right!' Bethany nodded her head, smiling.

'Hang on.' Lily tapped her on the shoulder. 'Here's Mr Lessing. We can ask him.'

Chloe would have preferred it to be almost anybody else. Mr Lessing was the one who had actually thought she'd set off the alarm! She shrank back behind Sara, looking scared.

'What's the matter?' For the first time, Sara actually sounded as though she wasn't regretting they'd ever seen Chloe the day before. Chloe looked so frightened, she couldn't help but feel sorry for her. 'Don't you like Mr Lessing?'

'I used to, but it was him who saw me, in the corridor. He went and told Ms Purcell about what I said on Friday as well,' Chloe whispered shakily. 'He really thinks it was me. Please can't we wait for someone else to find Miss James?'

'Don't be silly! We'll tell him it wasn't you,' Bethany said determinedly. Chloe was amazed how confident she sounded. After all, she was just about to tell one of her teachers that he was totally wrong. 'Mr Lessing! Can we talk to you, please?'

The drama teacher gave them a curious look, his eyes resting on Chloe for a long time. Then he turned back to Bethany. 'What is it?'

'You have to tell Ms Purcell that it wasn't Chloe who set off the alarm. It couldn't have been, you see – we saw her coming out of one of the practice rooms when the alarm went off. It must have been someone else.' Bethany beamed at him, and he couldn't help smiling back. 'I see,' he said slowly. 'You're sure?'

Bethany and Lily nodded vigorously, and Sara said, 'It definitely wasn't Chloe.'

Mr Lessing looked relieved. 'Good. Chloe, I'm really sorry – I didn't like thinking it was you, but I couldn't pretend I hadn't heard you on Friday – and then when I saw you . . . But I'm glad I was wrong.' He ran his hand through his hair, and shrugged. 'Of course, it doesn't help us with who actually *did* do it. But I'll go and see Ms Purcell now. Do you want to come, Chloe?'

Chloe was still feeling fragile. She *did* want to go, as she thought she wouldn't feel as though

everyone really believed her until she saw Ms Purcell again – but then . . .

'I think you should go,' Sara said unexpectedly. 'It's important.'

Chloe nodded slowly.

'Can we come too?' Bethany asked. 'Ms Purcell might want to see us anyway. We're Chloe's proof.'

'OK, let's go and see if she's in yet.'

Ms Purcell's secretary was there this time, and she gave Chloe a slightly disapproving look – which made Chloe certain that she needed to see the principal and get this all straightened out, or she'd be getting funny looks for ever. 'Ms Purcell's on the phone at the moment,' she said, smiling at Mr Lessing. 'But I'm sure she won't be long. If you wait, I'll tell her you're here when she gets off.'

Chloe plaited and unplaited her fingers nervously until at last they were told they could go in, and then they trooped through the door after Mr Lessing. Ms Purcell was sitting behind her desk looking thoughtful – and was it just Chloe's imagination, or was she also slightly embarrassed?

'Chloe, I don't know how to say this –'

'Please, Bethany and Lily and Sara saw me yesterday –'

They both stopped, and Ms Purcell smiled at her. 'Sorry, Chloe. I was going to say that I've just had a phone call from the council. They were digging up the road yesterday, and apparently they had an accident and hit some wires. Quite a few places round here have had electrical faults, so they were calling to let us know in case we'd been worried. No one set the alarm off at all! So obviously I owe you an apology.'

Chloe didn't know what to say. She hadn't quite imagined the principal apologising to her, somehow.

'That's brilliant, Chloe!' Bethany was grinning all over her face.

'And Chloe, I'll ring your parents now to let them know. You'd better get back to your form room, girls, it's nearly time for registration.'

As the door shut behind them, a slow smile spread over Chloe's face. Then she dropped her bag, and

threw her arms round Bethany. 'Thank you! Thank you! Thank you!' Then she waltzed on to hug Lily and Sara.

'But we didn't do anything!' Bethany protested laughing. 'Ms Purcell knew anyway.'

'You were going to, though. And after I was such a brat and got you in trouble in ballet. I'm so sorry about that, honestly.'

'We're going to be late,' Lily reminded them.

'What I want to know is,' said Sara as they set off upstairs, 'what were you doing in that practice room anyway? You don't have music lessons, do you?'

Chloe was silent for a minute, staring at the steps. Then she looked up at Sara. 'You'll laugh,' she said shyly. Then she sighed. 'I was practising singing. Not for a special lesson or anything. I was – well, hiding, I suppose.' She checked the others' faces, but they were just looking curious. 'It was after what you said about not having real friends, and showing off all the time. You were right. I mean, there was no way I was going to admit it at the time, but it was true. So I was staying out of the way of Sam and the

others. They're fun, but they're always doing stupid stuff, and then I get dragged into it too. Carmen and Ella mostly practise tap at lunch, so I didn't really have anyone else to hang around with. I know it sounds really sad,' she added, almost fiercely.

'It's not sad,' Sara said thoughtfully. 'You were just unlucky. I went overboard on the first day about the thing with Lizabeth. Lily thinks so too, don't you, Lils?'

'Mmm. You couldn't have known what she was saying to me. And Bethany told us that you got on really well at the audition.'

'If it hadn't been for Lizabeth, I'd definitely have come and found you on the first day,' Bethany agreed. 'She totally messed everything up!'

Chloe shuddered. 'I heard her talking about what she was going to do if she found out who set the alarm off. I think she's really evil! I hope Ms Purcell's going to say something about the alarm, otherwise she'll never leave me alone.'

Miss James beamed at Chloe as she came in, and

Chloe looked confused. She was so used to their form teacher not liking her!

'I've got an announcement, everyone. Ms Purcell has just told all the staff that the fire alarm was set off due to an electrical fault — no students were involved. Which is great, as now we don't have to worry about who did such a silly thing.'

Carmen squeaked and reached over her table to hug Chloe. 'I'm so sorry we thought it was you!'

'That's OK.' Chloe smiled back at her and Ella. 'I might have thought it was me too. If you see what I mean.'

Sam and his mates looked almost disappointed. 'Are they sure, Miss?' Jake asked. 'It was just an electrical thing?'

'Definitely.' Miss James nodded. 'And just don't get any ideas, Jake. You saw what trouble Chloe got into. Don't even think about it.'

It was the best morning Chloe had had at Lane's so far. All the staff seemed to be in a good mood, and for once Chloe didn't feel as though anyone was keeping an eye on her. She and Lily and Bethany

and Sara squashed themselves on to a lab bench with the twins for science, and managed to stay awake through Mrs Taylor's explanation of photosynthesis by having a competition to see who could make most words out of it. Then they went off in a giggly group for lunch – and Chloe didn't miss her little practice room at all.

Miss Jasper always arranged where they worked in ballet, so they were all split up, but Chloe felt so relaxed and happy that she danced brilliantly. She hadn't realised just how much feeling uptight had come out in her dancing. Miss Jasper even singled her out to show off her 'perfect' *battement tendu*. She went on and on about the great choreographer Balanchine, saying it was the most important exercise for a ballet dancer to learn, and Chloe glowed. It was even better when the others kept teasing her about it the whole time they were getting changed. Somehow Sara calling her Twinkletoes all the way to their jazz dance class just made her feel part of the group, and she loved it.

✳   ✳   ✳

Chloe couldn't wait to get home and see her mum – she was desperate to tell her about her fantastic day, especially after yesterday had been such a nightmare. So it was a real shock when Ms Purcell appeared in their form at the end of school. Chloe froze. Had the principal changed her mind? Did the staff think it was her who'd set the alarm off after all?

Bethany saw her stricken face and nudged her. 'Don't be such a muppet!' she whispered. 'She's not here because of you!'

Bethany was right. Ms Purcell was beaming, and looking particularly smug. She had a quick word with Miss James, and then stood at the front of the class, waiting for everyone to stop faffing about and listen to her. It took about thirty seconds. Then she smiled round at them all. 'This class is particularly lucky,' she purred. 'Usually it's at least a term before Lane's students get a professional audition –'

A gasp ran round the class. An audition? What for? Who was up for it?

Ms Purcell waited, still beaming, knowing she

had her audience in the palm of her hand. 'The whole of Years Seven and Eight are going to be seen by a casting team next week. A West End theatre is putting on a special Christmas run of *Mary Poppins* – and they're coming to Lane's to find the two child leads – one boy, one girl.' She laughed as the class exploded in delight. 'I'm sure you won't let us down. We'll have more details about it for you tomorrow.' And she sailed out, leaving them in an uproar.

'*Mary Poppins!*' Bethany yelped. 'That's my favourite musical ever!'

'Me too,' said Sara dreamily. 'Wouldn't it be brilliant if one of us got to be Jane Banks? In our first term!'

Chloe looked thoughtfully at her. 'You look right for it as well, Sara. They're bound to want someone who's blonde like the girl in the film.'

Sara grinned back at her. 'Ah, but they wouldn't want me, Chloe. Not when they could have someone who can do perfect *battement tendu*, the most important and boring ballet exercise ever invented. I mean, obviously you being ginger would be a

problem, but the production costs would probably run to a wig!' Then she ducked, giggling, as Chloe threw a pencil case at her.

'Which songs do the children sing?' Lily asked. 'I can't remember.'

Chloe and Sara stopped tussling, and thought.

'Do they have solos?' Sara asked. 'I think they join in on "A Spoonful of Sugar", and "Chim-Chim-Cheree". But I've only seen the film, not the stage version.'

'We'll find out tomorrow, probably,' Chloe put in. 'Did Ms Purcell really say next week? We're all being seen by a West End casting director *next week*?'

'Yup!' Bethany was trying to shrug on her coat, and hum "Feed the Birds", and dance at the same time without falling over. 'It's like a dream come true, isn't it?'

Chloe nodded. It really was. And she just couldn't wait for tomorrow.

Enjoy the other BRILLIANT and
fun-filled adventures in the

STAGE
School series!

Chloe was used to being the star of the class in her old school – always the funniest, brightest and most extrovert. But the *Marcia Lane School of Drama and Dance* is different. This isn't a place for showing off. All the pupils are stars in their own way. Will Chloe learn that acting the fool and being a good actress are not the same thing?

Sara is desperate to perform well in her audition for a leading role in ***Mary Poppins***, but Lizabeth, another talented student, has her eye on the same role and she is prepared to go to extremes to make sure the part is hers. Can Sara keep her cool and shine like a star?

Lily is used to pressure. Her mother is a famous actress and has always wanted Lily to follow in her footsteps. But Lily doesn't really want to be an actress – she wants to be herself. Then one day she gets the chance to audition for a fantastic part and she has to decide what she really wants. Is it too late to change her mind? Is there still time for her to become a STAR?

Bethany finds being a scholarship girl at the *Marcia Lane School of Drama and Dance* isn't that easy. Her long journey to school and the endless homework are hard enough, but on top of that she is trying to keep her scholarship secret. Then she gets the chance to perform in an exciting charity concert with world-famous Jasmine Day. But can Bethany cope with school and live her dream?

STAGE
School

Where Dreams Are Made!

Visit the sensational Stage School website for audition tips and quizzes at
www.bloomsbury.com/stageschool

'I'll help you and you'll help me,
For we are Sisters of the Sea!'

Look out for the new Arctica Mermaids series coming soon . . .

THE
DRAGON
DETECTIVE
AGENCY

Whatever your private detective needs, call **The Dragon Detective Agency** for a quick, reliable and flame retardant service.

RUBY ROGERS

OUT NOW . . .

COMING SOON . . .

AUGUST 2007

AUGUST 2007

Welcome to the world according to Ruby

To order any of these titles direct from
Bloomsbury Publishing visit
www.bloomsbury.com/bookshop
or call 020 7440 2475

BLOOMSBURY

www.bloomsbury.com